TITLE

CONFRONTING WRITER'S BLOCK

Chapter 1

Numb. That is the manner by which Kevin Corbett felt. He was latched onto his subconscious mind. Pondering the following passage. A creative slump was a revile. A dependable one that must be restored if even a word could jump out of his dim brown spiky hair.

His mocha eyes were drained. Worn from checking out at the screen of his PC. He murmured. Contemplating whether this was all worth the effort. Distributing harrowing tales had been a fantasy for him that was still too far. He submitted constantly his accounts to the site that he had the option to track down on the web crawler. Trusting that the organization would acknowledge one of his accounts. Be that as it may, come what may, it appeared as though they weren't allowing him an opportunity.

Ghastliness was the main point he could truly get into. He had endeavored different types yet they never felt right. He pummeled his clench hand against the work area. Overpowered with disappointment and pain. He shut his PC shut prior to heading first floor. He presented himself with a glass of bourbon in the kitchen. Drinking it gradually to appreciate what he could.

He glanced back at old recollections of his young life town. Golden Rivers. Where he had no companions and horrible guardians. However, he partook in the landscape there. It was moving. He nearly missed the spot. Necessary perhaps to go to get his creative mind train beginning once more? It wasn't a particularly far distance to get there. Only several hours.

He chose to take a risk and gather his sacks. After breakfast, he got in his vehicle. Heading to a town that he pondered had changed or remained something similar. The street before long became forlorn. Only the desert was near. His hold on the directing wheel fixed. Uncertain of the street he was taking. Something messed with him. He wished he understood what it was.

A huge corroded sign read out, 'Golden Rivers.' Some of the letters had blurred however were as yet sufficiently noticeable. He ended up shocked by the condition of the town. It looked like nobody had lived there for a really long time. The structures seemed deserted. Canvassed in soil, residue, spider webs, and anything uncommon stains were there. He swore he saw horrendous spots on different spots. He stopped at the parcel of an inn. He got out of the vehicle and glanced around.

In spite of being the final straggler, he felt like some other person or thing was with him. Perhaps products of something different. As though 1,000 eyes were on him. He tossed his jean coat on. Marshaling the mental fortitude to go into the inn, he tapped on the chime at the front work area. The ringing repeated. Uncovering how quiet it was. "Hi? Is anybody here?" No reaction came. He tapped the ringer once more. "Um excuse me? Might I at any point check in?"

Having stood by sufficiently lengthy, he took a key for 'Room 2.' He accumulated his gear from the vehicle and set them on the bed of his room. The room had two beds, a light, two drawers, a TV, a storeroom, a restroom, a telephone, and a window. He set his garments in the wardrobe. Hanging them there. He read through the menu that was on top of the TV. "I surmise I ought to check whether there's any food left."

Ground floor, the kitchen was behind the front work area. Its entry was that of two major entryways. He delicately pushed an entryway. Venturing into the faintly lit region where there were stuffing bubbling pots and spoiling food sources like vegetables, organic products, and meat. He hurried to the ovens. Turning them off before a potential fire could happen. He moaned out of alleviation. He whipped his head to the sound of something falling.

A can moved by. He followed where it had come from. A shut cooler. He advanced over to it. His unstable hand connected with the handle. He paused his breathing prior to opening the entryway. He panted at seeing hanging cleaned eyeless bodies. He covered his mouth. Doing his best not to smell the stinking aroma of the matured bodies. He scrammed out of the kitchen. Regurgitating when he left.

He cleaned the overabundance pieces of regurgitation with his sleeve. "I need to call somebody! I need to find support!" He snatched the telephone from the front work area. Dialing for police. The opposite side of the call quickly hit a steady repeating note. Never showing signs of change or getting any call. He hammered the telephone back on its holder. "Damn it!"

He froze at the breaking of glass and metal coming from outside. He jabbed his head out of the entryway. Seeing only his presently squashed vehicle. The windows were broken, the metal was twisted at all sides, and the tires were deprived of their air. Making the vehicle questionable. "What in the world?! Who might have done this?"

There was a reverberation of teeth chatting. It was far however close sufficient that he ran once more into the inn. Making a beeline for his room where he locked the entryway and pushed a cabinet against it. Keeping anything that it was outside from getting in. The entryway started to shake as the teeth chatting became stronger. He searched for any spot to stow away.

The entryway was kicked in. Breaking the cabinet and pieces of wood from the actual entryway. He kept a hand over his mouth. Under the bed, he watched cleaned legs and arms moving about. Searching for anything it desired. He perceived its appearance and contemplated whether the bodies he had found at the inn's kitchen were the very ones that were in his room. Some way or another combined. He could accept that there were three heads.

He shut his eyes at its wheezing and high pitch shouts. It sounded disappointed or held an outflow of timeless torment. A Skinned Crawler or Skinned Crawlers. With fast speed, it left the room. Moving further away. Leaving the inn. Horrendous foot and imprints denoted its presence.

Never allowing anybody to neglect.

Chapter 2

He slid out of the bed after what felt like long stretches of delaying. He tuned in for any clamors that would come from the Skinned Crawler. It was not even close to him. He crawled to the opened entryway. The entryway was slanted. Inclining at the side of the room with its pivots hanging out from their edges.

He stooped to get a superior glance at the horrendous hand and impressions. They didn't appear to be human looking. Like hands and feet with wound broken bones. Maybe disfigured. He left the room. Leaving the actual inn. He glanced around. Winding up dazed by obscurity. It was night. Some way or another. He stayed careful. Watching out for where he was.

Around the bend, there was an emergency clinic. Its structure was wide and tall. He got seeing light hair looking out from in the background of a window. It got away. "Is that...a individual? I keep thinking about whether they need assistance." He advanced toward the front entryways of the structure. He turned the handle. Opening the entryway gradually. Its material squeaked.

A virus wind blew the rotten papers that had been perched on the front work area where a medical caretaker would have been. Everything seemed to have been immaculate for quite a while. Very much like the inn. It was dim. No lights came from any bulbs. He got a spotlight which was on the floor. It looked new. He turned it on. Sparkling his direction to the left lobby. There were numerous entryways prompting perhaps different workplaces and spaces for patients.

"Hi? I saw you before. Do you really want any assistance?" The figure he was taking a gander at was female. Having long dark hair, a ridiculous medical clinic outfit, and fair skin. Its right hand had its finger bones standing out from tore tissue. Its left hand was that of a buzzsaw. "Miss?" It turned around. Uncovering that there was an eye on the buzzsaw. Its hair covered where its eyes potentially were. Its tongue was long. Looking like that of a snake's.

It murmured prior to swinging its saw at him. He hopped back and ran. Going to one side where there was a bunch of steps. His sweat-soaked palms sneaked off of the railing. His speedy feet sneaked off of a stage close to the highest point of the flight of stairs. Causing him to lose his equilibrium. Raising a ruckus around town. He could hear the Patient murmuring from behind. Drawing nearer. He constrained himself up. Swinging an entryway before himself open. Forcefully closing it with a speedy bit of the lock. Patient beat against the entryway. Letting out baffled murmurs. The metallic hints of its saw repeated. Inside a second, it surrendered. Leaving the entryway. He slowed down to rest. He shakily went for the gold the corridor he was in. Tracking down additional entryways. "Imagine a scenario where there are a greater amount of them?" There were weighty strides. He covered his mouth. Listening unobtrusively. It didn't seem like a Patient. Whoever being wearing shoes was appeared. Not taking risks, he ran a few doors down. Arriving at the entryway toward the end which he opened. There was a sitting area. Old magazines thronw about the room. The seats were broken, rotten, lost, or appropriately staying there. A variety of dusty outlined photos were slanted and stained with blood.

He panted at a dribbling sound. Understanding that he had ventured over a puddle of blood which he made a stride back from. He focused the light above. Showing balancing digestive organs over the main ceiling fixture. Choking, he made a beeline for two major entryways. There were carcasses covered with ridiculous stained sheets. Their long hair looked like fairly natural. Obviously this was a Surgery Room.

He moved the light to the bodies. Thinking about how this even occurred in any case. For what reason was everybody dead? Also, how did the beasts of Amber Rivers became? He wished there was a survivor. Somebody who could clear up everything for him. Yet, it looked like he was separated from everyone else in a not so deserted town where terrifying beasts existed exclusively to benefit from the scraps of the past.

He needed to leave however something told him in any case. Like it was his obligation to figure out reality. Furthermore, where it counts, he acknowledged that thought since this was once his home. In any event, when the majority of the late individuals here were never good to him as a kid, he actually had some affection for the town. A feeling of kinship with the trees and blossoms. Nature was a preferable companion over humankind. It didn't mean he needed something like this to reoccur. Indeed, even with dread structure up inside himself, he constrained himself to hold strolling to an entryway opposite the careful room.

The cadavers sat up from their metal beds. He gradually turned. The sheets delicately tumbled off. Uncovering a column of Patients. His shoe hit a truck. Thumping a handgun to the floor. He got it. Pointing it at the running Patients. He terminated at them. Taking some out prior to hurling himself entirely into the following room. Closing the entryway. Patients beat against the entryway. Effectively slicing through the material. He hopped back. Proceeding to run until he notice an opened entryway. He jumped into the janitor's wardrobe. Closing and locking the entryway.

He sat at a corner. Turning the light off, he held up in obscurity. Patients wrecked an entryway. Running a few doors down. Their murmuring turned out to be more far off until there was stunned quietness. He put his assets on the floor.His flimsy hands covered his dreaded articulation. Wailing.

"That is not who I am any longer. That is not me..."

Chapter 3

He held the firearm. Gazing at it. "Individuals actually view at me as though I'm as yet that equivalent individual. I can see it in their eyes. I realize they can't stand me. Am I a quitter for not expressing anything by any means?" He brushed his fingers over the metal.

"For what reason am I even here? Dislike anybody at any point loved me. They scorned me. Utilized me like their own punching pack." He embraced his knees. "This town most likely doesn't need me. I'm certain of it." He looked at the entryway. "However at that point for what reason am I stuck here?"

He glanced around. "A slip-up. That is who I am. I shouldn't be alive." He carried the firearm to his head. "Should help everybody out." There was a thump at the entryway. He brought down the weapon. Gazing at the entryway. Another thump. He stood. Squeezing himself against it. "Hi? Is somebody there?" ,asked the secret voice. "Indeed. Who are you?" "I'm Doctor Lydia. What's your name?" "...Kevin." "Kevin. Alright. Is it safe to say that you are okay? Do you want any assistance?" "I-I'm fine. I don't believe I'm harmed."

"Are you certain?" He didn't answer. "How about you open the entryway? I can surrender you a check." "Are those things...around?" "What? What are you referring to?" "Those beasts. They pursued me down. I scarcely got out alive." "How about you draw me an image and afterward I'll be aware?" The lock clicked! He gradually opened the entryway. Seeing the specialist before him.

She had short light hair, blue eyes, and red lips. Wearing a sterile garment, dim red neck sweater, and some khaki jeans.

She put her hand on his arm. "Here we go. I'll take you to my office." He slipped the weapon under his jeans. Keeping a hold of the electric lamp.

His things were on the work area in her room. He sat at the foot of a clinical bed. Allowing her to inspect him. He flickered whenever she was finished focusing a little light in his eyes. "You are by all accounts fine. What's more, you said you saw a few beasts?" She got the drawing of a Patient. "Indeed I did. They were attempting to kill me. I don't have any idea what they are nevertheless they don't need us here." "How do you have any idea that?" "I don't. Possibly I'm correct or they simply kill anybody they see." She concentrated on the drawing prior to shaking her head. "Please accept my apologies Mr. Corbett yet you should be under a great deal of pressure. I've seen nothing like this in the area."

"Might it be said that you are messing with me?! Take a gander at where you are! This spot is deserted! For what reason would you say you are even still here?!" "Deserted? This spot is as yet flourishing." "No, it's not! I tracked down bodies at the inn! As far as we might be aware, everybody's dead!" She lifted her hands. "Quiet down. You said you tracked down bodies at the inn? We ought to go report this to the police."

He gripped his head. Gritting his teeth. "You're not paying attention to me! You don't get it!" She opened the top bureau. Taking out a container of pills. Giving them to him. "Take two of these regularly in the first part of the day. You'll be fine." She left the room with the drawing. He read over the printed words on the jug. He contorted the top open. Taking out two pills. Reluctantly, he threw the pills in his mouth. Gulping them dry.

He stuffed the container in his coat pocket prior to jumping off of the bed. Passing on the room and following the signs to the exit. He let out a murmur of help when he saw the roads. His alleviation immediately went to stress. "Lydia?" He panted at seeing a dead body. He bowed. Inspecting the cadaver. He shook his head. "No. It's not her but...when did this unfortunate charlatan appear? For what reason did he...?"

There was a reverberating of teeth prattling. He ran the other way. Never thinking back. His chest felt like it was consuming. Breathing intensely with a sharp aggravation on his side. He saw the opened entryways of a primary school. He raged inside. Closing the entryways and putting the lock over it. He had no key to get out. In any case, he was appreciative that it couldn't get in.

He fell to his knees. Pausing to rest. Tears ran down his cheeks. He covered his face. Stressed over seeing something different. "Sir! I can't find my teddy bear. Will you assist me with tracking down it?" He went to the young man's voice. All he saw was a teddy bear. Sitting on the floor close to him. He got it. Not a single kid was to be found. "I don't have the foggiest idea who recently talked however I ought to go search for them. It's undependable for anybody to become mixed up in a spot like this."

He stuffed the bear in his back pocket.

With his weapon close by, he advanced a few doors down. Something sparkly got his attention. It was a rack at the end. One with columns of prizes and decorations. Outlined photos of those associated with the contests stayed there as well. He put a hand on the transparent glass. "They generally anticipated that I should accomplish something with my life. Getting some information about school and occupations when I was just eight. That is the point at which I understood that I had no fantasies. I'm under water now." He rested his head up against the glass.

"That is the reason " There was an unexpected accident of what seemed like work areas being pushed over.

He raised the weapon. Strolling to the entryway that read, 'Math.' The entryway gradually opened. He went for the gold the study hall. Work areas were dispersed about. Splatters of blood was all over the place. There were conditions on the blackboard. Biting and grinding of tissue were extremely near hear. Following the sounds, he halted.

Many decaying heads were approaching over the body of a young man. They had insect legs, screwy broken teeth, ragged looking eyes, and two mouths. The Lingerers stopped. Gradually going themselves to where the light was coming from. His unstable firearm focused on them. They ran at him with blood and torn tissue swinging from their mouths. He shouted.

Bang! Bang! Bang!

Chapter 4

Lingerers laid about with shot openings implanted in them. Their blood stained the floor. Their tissue was for all intents and purposes mush as their legs stood out. He was shrouded in their blood. He stooped by the young man's side. He took out the teddy bear.

"I never got an opportunity at a youth. Not actually. Things moved so quick for me. It resembled the world believed me should grow up as of now. I want to have halted it." He set the bear in the young man's arms prior to leaving the study hall. He shut the entryway. "Please accept my apologies. I was unable to save you."

He pushed the enormous entryways of an exercise center. The wooden deck was canvassed in shape. It was moist and fragmented. The b-balls sitting on the racks had abruptly skipped. Meaning to him. He covered his head. Giving his all to protect himself. In any case, many got to him. He pushed himself into one of the restrooms. Locking the entryway. Thorned wires emerged from the roof. Getting him by his wrists and lower legs. Taking him off the floor. He battled to free himself yet it just made it simple for the wires to slice through his skin. Blood dribbled from his cuts.

"No! Let me go! If it's not too much trouble, just let me go! I'll leave! I guarantee I will!" The wires maneuvered him into the obscurity above. "NO!"

He panted conscious. Sitting promptly up. He glanced around. "Stream. It's the river..." A virus breeze ran past him. Delicate grass laid under him. The waters streamed with incredible quiet. He checked his wrists and lower legs yet found no such injuries that could review prior occasions. He stood. "I use to come here at times." He strolled over. "This stream was well known for individuals who suffocated themselves here. After school, I would descend here and envision myself conversing with them. Individuals who passed on here. Inquiring as to why they got it done. Once in a while, I contemplated suffocating as well. However, I was consistently terrified of water. With the exception of this one. I'm as yet apprehensive yet this river..."

He gazed back at his own appearance. "It's extraordinary."

He connected. Allowing the water to contact his fingers. A shout repeated. He whipped his head to its sound. "Huh?! What in the world was that? Is somebody in harm's way?" A lady in a wedding dress with long dark hair was peering down as she strolled towards him. She held a bunch of yellow roses. "Are you alright?" He moved forward. "Who are you?"

La Muerta lifted her head. Her eye cosmetics was dribbling. As though she had been weeping for such a long time. She wailed prior to letting out another shout. He took off. Trusting he would find a protected spot away from her. He may as yet hear her cries. Drawing nearer and closer. He stumbled over a stone. Raising a ruckus around town. "Ugh!" He propelled himself up. Investigating the distance of where she had once been. It appeared as though she was no more.

He went to the gravestone. His eyes extended at seeing it. Perusing the name that was engraved on stone.

Daisy Derrickson

His head brought down. "It wasn't my issue. You had a medical issue. I actually lament our last second together. We were contending. I didn't believe that that should be my last memory of you. I never maintained that you should consider me a terrible individual before you passed on. In all actuality we were never companions. We scarcely knew one another." He brushed his hand over her name. "I was at your burial service. Loved ones were permitted to be there. My close buddy drove me there. He realized you better."

Tears hit the texture of his pants. Staining them. "Indeed, even the educators knew you." He grasped the grass. "I felt unwanted at that congregation. As I didn't have a place. Their eyes were all on me. They were irate with me. I simply know it." He folded his arms over her gravestone. Crying. "I miss you. Regular I do. I can always remember. It's killing me." He laid on his side. Confronting her gravestone. "Yet, presently I realize that it was never my shortcoming. It will undoubtedly work out."

Gradually, he shut his eyes.

He moaned. Upset by the hard wood under him. He sat up. Ending up confronting a huge cross that was nailed to the wall. An opened casket laid before it. "How did I...?" He shook his head. "I ought not be here." Low wails could be heard coming from the opened final resting place. He made cautious strides over.

The lady was laying there. She didn't move nor talked. All in all, where did the cries come from? His face met hers. "Daisy..." He put his hands on the edge of the final resting place. His head brought down. "Please accept my apologies."

Her hand jerked prior to connecting. He panted. Staggering back. She grasped the side of the casket. Sitting up from its help. She turned her head. Her mouth opened wide. A sadness stricken articulation laid on her wonderful veil. Ridiculous tears dribbled down her cheeks. She let out a crushed shout. Drifting high hanging out there with a bunch of yellow roses in her grasp.

He hurried to the front entryways of the congregation. He contorted the handle however found the entryways impeded by something. He propelled himself against the entryways. Without any result, it wouldn't open. Daisy traveled to him. As yet shouting. The bouquet was tossed at his bearing. A haze of dust burst. He covered his nose. Taking off from the dust's bedtime song. Thumping himself against the opened book where marks had been composed there in pen. A shotgun laid over it.

He snatched the weapon. Daisy tossed the blossoms once more. He leaped far removed. Stirring things up around town with a snort. He pointed and pulled the trigger. She shouted at the hot metal in her chest. His tears dazed him. He brought down the weapon. "Simply pay attention to me! We should talk! We don't need to do this!"

She flew towards him. Making the breeze blow emphatically. He shut his eyes. His flimsy finger pushed against the trigger. Bang!

He heard a body hit the floor. His eyes gradually opened. Dropping the weapon, he covered his mouth at seeing Daisy's body. He tumbled to his knees. Wailing over her.

Chapter 5

He constrained himself to take her body off the floor. Giving his all to stroll to the casket where he put her there. Keeping the bouquet in her grasp. He shut the final resting place prior to getting the shotgun.

Removing a few stages, he halted. Turning his head. "Goodbye..."

Out of the congregation, he wound up still in the town. Across the road, there was a line of organizations. Like the ones on the road he remained on. He froze. Hearing the hints of something hauling against the street. A middle had its digestion tracts hanging out from behind. A path of blood followed it. The impression of its ribcage was noticeable. A foot hung out from its neck stump which was loaded up with a mind.

The Foot Dragger developed nearer. Kevin made a stride back. His shoe scratched itself against the asphalt. The animal halted. It pushed its hands against the ground prior to running towards the sounds. He shot the weapon. The Foot Dragger detonated into a variety of body parts. His legs were like jam. He covered his mouth. Choking at the frightful sight.

He opened up the pill bottle. Unloading a couple of pills in his mouth prior to pausing to rest. More Foot Draggers went along. He yelled, "I can't stand you! I disdain you!" He ran not too far off. The Foot Draggers followed behind. His eyes got a coffee shop with gleaming red letters. He crushed the glass entryways with the handle of the weapon. He put his hand through the hole. Turning the lock.

He stared at the hatchet that was encased in glass for crises. Befuddled by its presence. However, he crushed the glass. Snatching the hatchet. The Foot Draggers developed nearer. He let out a disappointed shout as he strike. Bringing the sharp point against their bodies. In spite of their endeavors to kick, they were no counterpart for such quick outrage. Their blood finished the walls, deck, and furniture. Bits of themselves stacked up over one another.

His garments were stained with their blood. His face held signs of it as well. He paused to rest when he understood they were dead. The hatchet dropped out of his hand. "I HATE YOU! Don't bother ME!"

He whipped his head to what laid behind him. His hair remained on their closures. He saw the town's grin. He could hear its chuckling. Insulting him that his destiny could never show signs of change.

A Foot Dragger kicked his head. Taking him out. He gradually opened his eyes after an obscure measure of time. Viewing where he was as lit. He gradually stood. Viewing the heap of hacked bodies as gone. That the cafe was like it was previously. At the point when he would arrive at this spot for a burger and pop. Eating with Lydia.

"Lydia...You were there. In any case, how are you still here? Like this? For what reason didn't you leave?" Heels clicked against the floor. He pivoted. Confronting Lydia who held a plate of hamburgers and French fries with drinks. She grinned. "Could we eat? You should be ravenous."

Both sat opposite one another at a table. "You utilized me. You constrained me to take these damn drugs!" "I never constrained you to do anything. I gave you a choice and you took it. What you did after that was all you." "And for what reason would it be a good idea for me to trust you? All you specialists think something similar! They generally called me insane! No one important who might just converse with the headstones of Amber Rivers Cemetery."

Lydia opened a ketchup bundle. Pressing out a little heap of the red glue. She dunked a fry in it. "Do you recollect when you let me go with you? To the graveyard? You were eager to find another person who was keen on your leisure activities. I partook in the minutes we had. It resembled having a child." Kevin grimaced. He gazed at his food. "My folks were horrible to me. They would rebuff me for things that I assumed I had fouled up. In some cases, I keep thinking about whether I am still off-base. Yet, you showed me that they were beasts."

He stopped. "You were my actual mother."

She put her hand on his. He checked her out. "I'm glad for you for having come this far." She remained from her seat. They went to the windows of the cafe. Watching the haze develop as downpour poured from the dim sky. "Here and there you'll require individuals like me and that is fine. Here and there, you will not. Furthermore, that is fine as well." She left the burger joint. He followed her however halted at the entry. Watching her stroll through the thick haze. Becoming doused by its tears.

The thick mist vanished. The downpour reached a sluggish stop. Specialist Lydia Hassan had left.

Kevin contemplated whether he could at any point see her once more. Did he have the right to see her? He looked at the note on the floor. Perusing it over when he got it.

The Wisdom of Teeth

It fills spirits with a sort of toxic substance

To insult those that know nothing about their agony

Strolling obliviously down the road while a hand keeps on coming to

Taking them to the trees so they might figure out how to tie a bunch

He raised a forehead. "For what reason does this vibe incomplete?" He got out of the cafe. Strolling in profound idea. "Taking them to the trees...To tie a bunch? Like the forest? I wasn't there. Not actually. Perhaps I missed something? It'll assist me with completing the sonnet."

He collapsed the paper. Setting it in his pocket. He headed down a street. Hearing the leaves and their calls.

Write..

Chapter 6

The woods held a forlorn touch. Kevin strolled. Searching for whatever appeared to be awkward. Something brushed against the parts of the trees. Its leaves talked. He halted. Hearing intently.

A cadaver leaped out from the tree close to him. Hanging by a thick rope that was attached to the tree. The cadaver had dark skin. Its arms and legs were out. Wearing only a dark trash container as it held a sharp pencil. Smiling with sharp teeth and wide eyes.

Hanged Writers.

More showed up from different trees. Chuckling as they motioned the pencil as though they were cutting somebody with them. The Hanged Writer before him had focused all over. He lifted a hand. His hand was punctured by the weapon. Draining from a cut. "Ok!" He grasped his hand. Running off from the area. Hanged Writers showed up any place he went.

His shoe slipped on mud. Falling into the huge opening. His shouts repeated.

It had been hours. He didn't know what time it was. In any case, he realize that he was as yet alive. He focused the light in obscurity room. Standing and pausing for a minute to inspect where he was. He recoiled at the horrible scents. Waving his hand at them. He took out the collapsed paper which was presently doused from the sewage water. "No! The sonnet! It's demolished!" He coarseness his teeth. Tossing the clustered wet paper ball away. He focused to his left side and right. "Where in the world am I expected to go?"

A high pitch shout repeated. He turned. "What in the world?! What was that?" He tuned in for some other commotions however heard nothing else. He before long followed where the shout was.

The walls were made of such thick soil. No man-made object was around until he had arrived at a corroded entryway. He gradually opened it. There was a room loaded up with clinical devices and books. A bed held a carcass that been cut up into pieces. The individual's head had been set so it confronted the entryway. Its middle remained close to it while its appendages were heaped on top of one another.

He kept his eyes on the frightening sight as he advanced toward the entryway across the room. With his back turned, he curved the handle however halted when he heard something hit the floor. He faltered prior to meeting the producer of the commotion. It was a head without its skin. Its eyes remained. Gazing at him. It had a wreck of brown long hair with scarcely much strands yet a fix or here there. It transformed into a Lingerer.

Breathing intensely, he kicked the animal. Sending it across the room where it hit a stopping point. Pushing over some glass holders. It caused a scene. Some white fluid had spilled from one the containers. Consuming into its tissue.

He opened the entryway up. Hurling himself entirely into the entryway and forcibly closing the entryway. Contorting its lock. He sparkled the spotlight on what seems to be a recreation area. It hoped to be deserted. Canvassed in a flood of grass. The jungle gym gear was corroded. The seats were worn and rotten. There was a wellspring in the center. Dimness covered the region. An odd light kept the recreation area noticeable.

He strolled over. Looking into the waters. He shouted. Dropping the light and punching the water. Endeavoring to break his appearance. Yet, regardless of how frequently he did, his appearance remained. He fell to his knees. Slowing down to rest. A thump repeated. He got his light. Sparkling it on an entryway that was unexpectedly there. It had the number '13' cut into it at the top. An animation rendition of a phantom sat underneath it. He endeavored to open the entryway yet thought that it is locked. The number disappeared as did the apparition. An unnerved horrendous face with protruding eyes framed on the wood. Not red paint. He suspected as much. He could see now that it was blood that had been utilized to make this astonishing picture.

He saw how gleaming the eyes were. Sawdust was hanging close by. The eyes...They were genuine. Chills ran down his spine. He was unable to remove his eyes from the entryway. Stressed that something would kill him assuming he turned away. He attempted the entryway once more. Thinking that it is shockingly opened. The closures of those eyes were hanging. He shut his eyes.

Something drove him into the room. He hit the floor. Wincing at the hard wood. The entryway forcefully closed. He saw his appearance all over. A child's cry repeated. Turning out to be clearly and more tormented. He covered his ears. "Stop it! Make it stop!" He terminated at the mirrors which drained. The crying had halted. He rested up against the entryway. Bending the handle, he battled before the entryway opened. He got himself.

The recreation area had kids messing about. He seemed to be back in the town. "Hello! What are you all doing here? This town's loaded with beasts!" Their heads turned. Every one of them held a similar face. They fairly looked like that of the dead youngster he had tracked down in the school.

Teeth prattling reverberated somewhere far off. It developed ever nearer. The children shouted as Skinned Crawler started tearing them separated with the mouth that was behind it. It had a hand standing out of its mouth. Snatching kids and tossing them in. Kevin ran off. Heading into the washrooms. He locked a slow down. Reloading his firearm, he kept it close. Hanging tight for it to follow.

Two feet became noticeable on the opposite side. There was a thump. "Hi? Is it true that anyone is in there? You dropped something." "Who are you? How are you even here?" "I don't know yet I go by Phoenix Greenwood. I found this container of medication and accepted it was yours." He opened the entryway. Encountering a sharp looking man who had an eyepatch over his left eye, short dark hair, and a noticeable blue eye.

He looked him over. "You look natural. Have I seen you some place?" "I don't have any idea yet I've never seen you." He acknowledged the jug. "Indeed, much appreciated. I can't lose this." "I envision it's vital to you." He saw the scar on his cheek. His eyes augmented. "What is it?"

"It's you!"

Chapter 7

"In this way, you came here for motivation?" ,asked Phoenix. "No doubt. I don't have the foggiest idea. It sounds moronic." "Not to me."

They were strolling down the road.

"Be that as it may, it is. This town can't stand me. None individuals considered me to be me. In school, I was being tormented and my folks were no greater than them. All I could possibly do was stay alone." He scowled. "Assuming you and I had gone to a similar school, I would have shown you how to battle." "Indeed, it's past the point of no return for that." He shook his head. "Guarding yourself is rarely past the point of no return. Individuals once considered me to be an insane person with such a handicap that held me back from doing anything. Some actually do. However, generally, I'm viewed as a supernatural occurrence. Or on the other hand a man of solidarity with an endearing personality. I like that portrayal better."

"In any case, you didn't even let those individuals know that. They found out by committing errors." "Yes yet they likewise figured out through those that gave me regard. I had never implied those individuals. However, they considered me to be an individual. I'm thankful to find the people who will give reality."

Kevin halted. So did he. Raising a forehead at him. Kevin folded his arms. He peered down. "Phoenix? Have you at any point thought about...killing somebody? I know it's terrible however I did once. At the point when I was in that school, I was unable to quit pondering wounding them. My harassers. Indeed, even my folks. In any case, I never made it happen. I would never make it happen. I'm excessively frightened to. Also, the responsibility would kill me." He shut his tear-filled eyes. "I presumably sound like a beast to you."

Phoenix laid a hand behind him. Kevin gazed toward him. "Not by any stretch. I can kind of comprehend where your coming from. Seriously. There are times when I wanted to hit somebody for being a self-important ass. Be that as it may, once in a while, you need to resist the urge to panic. In the event that it helps, I could track down a specialist for you." Kevin took out the container. "I previously had one. She gave me these yet they're beginning to break down." "Then, at that point, we'll find another specialist for you who can give you something different. One specialist is rarely enough." Phoenix grinned. "This isn't an ideal end for you. It's just the start."

Kevin apprehensively held his sleeve. "Can I...hug you?" Phoenix gestured. Kevin tenderly brought his arms around him. Squeezing his head against his chest. Crying there. However Phoenix had possibly embraced somebody while a staggering circumstance had happened very much like the numerous men residing in the old neighborhood that he was in. He made this exemption in light of the fact that the conditions that they were in. Furthermore, he knew the sort of aggravation that he felt. He had experienced a few difficulties as well.

"I don't know what to do now. I assume I need to leave yet there's a section that is letting me know that I need to remain and track down something." ,said Kevin when the embrace broke. "What do you imagine that is?" He shrugged. "I don't know. Everything's befuddling now. I simply wish Lydia was still here." "Then, at that point, perhaps you want to recall something so you can track down something? What about the exhibition hall?" "I rather not." His eyes broadened at seeing a toy store.

Phoenix hurried to it. Finding Kevin running towards the extravagant creatures. Playing with them. Imagining that they were talking. "You're taking off from your concerns. This is never going to fix anything and you know it. You need to make the wisest decision for yourself." "And how would you anticipate that I should do that?!" Kevin glared. "You've had to deal with some horrible things you actually got back up and approached your life! I couldn't in fact do that!" "You don't have to endure a damaging occasion to become gallant." "I'm not requesting that you dispose of parts of my mind! I'm trying to say can any anyone explain why you can simply do anything you set your psyche as well, however when I attempt to do anything I break into pieces and come up short?!"

"Kevin-" He stood. Dropping the toys. "Individuals take a gander at you and they see a supernatural occurrence of science! A certain man without any concerns on the planet. You're viewed as a legend with such alluring highlights. A legend in the books. Everybody loves you." He dismissed. Grasping his arms. "Nobody considers you to be an oddity. Be that as it may, nothing happened to me and everybody considers me to be one."

"You know the entire story, right?" ,asked Phoenix. Kevin wheezed. "Uh Yeah." "Then, at that point, you know how this occurred. Since you realize that this was a mishap. In the event that it hadn't been for my moronic mix-ups, I wouldn't have this injury by any means. So it was exclusively by sheer karma that anybody has a ton of familiarity with what's inside our heads as a result of me. In any case, I wasn't pleased with how they treated those horribly defenseless individuals later on. They took what has been going on with me and degraded it."

He turned at Phoenix who showed some mistake. "While I caused a few advantages, I likewise made hurt. One way or the other, it was a mishap. I never arranged it. Very much like you never arranged your future as what it is. We have zero control over everything except whatever might be possible. I had the option to keep a task even after the shocking occurrence. That's what since I knew whether I laid there in distress, I would just be harming myself."

Kevin cleared a few removes. He made a sound as if to speak. "Might we at any point go see the historical center?" Phoenix opened the entryway for him. "I'll lead the way."

Down the road, Kevin said, "Did you at any point catch wind of the talk that you unexpectedly turned out to be physically dynamic? Like an insane sum?" Phoenix chuckled so hard that his face went red. He slapped his knee. "That gossip never goes downhill!"

Kevin unexpectedly thought of himself as snickering. Feeling this wonderful warmth in his chest.

Chapter 8

The two men were remaining before the exhibition hall. "All things considered, this is where I leave." ,said Phoenix. "Huh? What are you referring to? I thought you were accompanying me?" "I directed you here yet presently I want to return home. Furthermore, you want to confront this by itself." "Yet where are you going?" "To Osburn Oaks." "Osburn Oaks? That is the burial ground."

Phoenix gestured happily. "It is." He removed a few stages prior to halting. "Ya know, it's sort of unusual to say this yet I had eyes only for you when I saw your photos." ,said Kevin. Phoenix laughed. "I'll accept that as a commendation. Farewell now."

Kevin directed his concentration toward the large entryways before him. Hearing his strides becoming far off. He anxiously scoured his arm prior to opening an entryway. Entering the dusty old spot.

The relics and old photographs grabbed his eye. Making him strolled towards them. There was an image of a couple remaining close to a destitute haven. They were one of a handful of the who were known in the past for their liberality. The garments on the photograph were saved on life sized models in encased glass cases. He glared. "I can't stand this town! I can't stand you! I disdain you!" He pushed over the glass cases. They broke into pieces. The life sized models lost their appendages. Dust rose from the old garments.

He removed a piece of the photograph from the casing. "When has this town at any point helped me?! When has anybody at any point dealt with me like an individual?" He took the casing off. Swinging it at a portion of different relics. Breaking numerous things as he tossed what he could. He halted when it appeared as though there was sufficient harm. Shaking, tears moved from his eyes. He tumbled to his knees. Letting out a baffled shout.

He noticed an image that was on the ground close to his hands. It was Phoenix Greenwood. The one who had showed science that there was something else to the mind besides they had initially thought. He held the photograph close. His heart sank at how he had treated the authentic things. He collapsed the image and stuffed it in his pocket. He strolled into the other room which had wax sculptures. He ventured over to the Grim Reaper sculpture. Pressing a red button that was beneath its jaw.

There was a tick sound prior to something opened. Behind him, a piece of the wall had slid over. Uncovering a secret entryway. He reluctantly opened the entryway. Loaded up with a weighty feeling of fear in his chest.

On the steps, there were kids who had dissolved tissue hauling behind. Their skeletal parts were fairly apparent. Hauling themselves towards him with tormented cries. He shouted. One of them snatch his lower leg. He started it off. Running past them and down the steps. He slipped on a stage. Falling until he arrived at the base floor. He moaned. Constraining himself to remain as he gripped his head. Resting up against the wall. He saw his ridiculous hand.

The youngsters appeared to be tranquil. Had they left? Or on the other hand would they say they were pausing? He focused the light a few doors down. Seeing ways on his left side and right. He paused his breathing at seeing Skinned Crawler. It remained there. Gazing at him. Never moving. "Quit checking me out! Don't bother me!" It let out low wheezes and groans. Where its butt ought to have been was a mouth with two sharp tooths and a hand standing out of there. The tooths clicked together. Making the very babbling sounds that he had heard in the roads.

It ran towards him. Wasting now is the right time. Leaving huge breaks. He opened an entryway up. Hurling himself in the room prior to closing the entryway. Locking it. Shockingly, it didn't endeavor to follow.

A hacking fit got away from his lips. The spotlight dropped out of his hand. He dropped to his knees. Squeezing his hands against the wood as pieces of blood finished the floor. The hacking developed further. Practically like it was punching his chest. A razor leaped out of his mouth. Laying in a little puddle of blood. He gripped his neck. "How the hell...?" He slowed down to rest.

He focused the light into the room. It seemed to be a little library. They seemed, by all accounts, to be books dating before present day times. He strolled over to the rack close to him. Skimming through the titles that were on the spines of these books. Some had to do with clinical information, centers around plants, expressive insights concerning nature, and different kinds of subjects.

A book tumbled off of a rack. He whipped his head to a book that was on floor close to one of the racks. Going beyond a couple, he got the book. Perusing it. "The Mentally Deranged Of Amber Rivers." He flipped through the pages. Searching for whatever was like what he knew. He panted at seeing his youngster self. An image of him remaining close to the trees. This photograph ought to have been private. How could it arrive?

"My parents...They gave this to them." Memories streaked through his head. "Presently I recall. They made me go take treatment when they found me conversing with trees." He shook his head. Closing his eyes. "Not trees. There was a body. It was in a trash container. Somebody...Somebody killed them. For reasons unknown, I wasn't frightened. I recently held conversing with the body. Why?"

A glimmer of light dazed him. The book dropped out of his grasp. Raising a ruckus around town. He squeezed the edge of his nose. "I use to converse with dead bodies. Since no other person would converse with me. It actually has neither rhyme nor reason. I might have conversed with creatures or toys. For what reason did it need to be bodies?"

At the opposite side of the room, there was an entryway. Reverberations of banging could be heard. Its pivots were losing its solidarity. The wood fragmented and bowed. The entryway fell. A Foot Dragger was advancing toward him. Having heard the commotions. He discharged yet just a single shot came. It started moving quick. He ran into the entryway that it had come from.

A shocking tune repeated. He shouted out. Having heard it once a long time back. Reviewing seeing spoiling cadavers and a blade. A man was holding it. The man checked him out. Grinning. "Gracious god! It was him! I conversed with him without knowing! Without getting it! Also, he let me go close to them!"

The Clover Killer was a man in his twenties who delighted in wounding his casualties to death. Leaving their bodies in the forest. Nonetheless, there were times when he killed somebody an alternate way. The main way the police had the option to connect these homicides to him was a result of the clovers that he would abandon. Clovers that generally possessed an aroma like pumpkin.

For what reason did he allow Kevin to live?

Chapter 9

Kevin reloaded his firearm in a janitor's storage room. He kept his light off. Pausing.

Foot Dragger developed nearer. Moving any place it assumed it expected to go. He covered his mouth. Pausing his breathing. It appeared to be all the more further away. He paused to rest. Allowing himself to unwind briefly.

Lament made him inexpressibly pleased. Wishing he had recently remained at home. Or then again had viewed one more way as enlivened. He took a look out the entryway. Checking assuming that anything was near. He ventured out when he made his judgment. The floor broke under him. He shouted. Falling into murkiness. His eyes opened a second after the fact. He painstakingly stood. It seemed like he hadn't broken anything.

"How could I be even alive? That fall ought to have killed me."

His mouth expanded open at seeing artistic creations of himself having kicked the bucket in numerous ways. Every one of them appear to be self-incurred. "Who drew these? Nobody knows me. Why would...Why would anybody do this?" He took a gander at the weapon in his grasp then, at that point, gazed toward the composition of himself with a firearm to his head. He strolled over to it. Bringing down the canvas to uncover a square formed opening. There was a red key in it.

He stuffed it in his pocket.

Through the spoiling entryway, he was met with a corridor. There weren't an excessive number of ways to glance through. Only a couple were along the way. He actually look at some. Viewing a couple as difficult to open. Some held ammunition. In the end, he arrived at the last entryway. The one shrouded in tissue. It didn't take him one moment to figure what key would open it. Be that as it may, he wavered. Contemplating whether he could do this.

Might he at some point confront them?

The least demanding way out of this would be a shot to his head. However, he contemplated the individuals who urged him to develop. He understood that he had kept himself alive. Never relinquishing his ongoing objective. Endurance.

His heart hustled with each move he made to open the entryway. When the entryway was opened, he could see that the enormous room was worked out of a similar material as the entryway. There was a lofty position against the wall. Looking opposite him. Cleaned Crawler stayed there. Watching him yet never endeavoring to move. He ventured into the room. From all sides, he was met with each beast that he had found around here. Their appearances were presently his. He gripped his head and shut his eyes. Shouting at the sight.

They made nearer strides. He coarseness his teeth. Realizing that he needed to make it happen. That he was unable to let this be his destiny. He frowned at them. "I don't require you! I needn't bother with any of you! Not a solitary one of you are significant! Not any longer!" He took a full breath. "I acknowledge you all as you are nevertheless you took care of your responsibilities."

The animals froze. Liquefying on the spot until they were puddles of their previous selves.

He gazed toward Skinned Crawler. "You! You've tormented everybody sufficiently far! Descend here and battle!"

Cleaned Crawler shrieked prior to arriving on the ground. His clench hands gripped. "You're only a weakling. Carrying everybody down with your damn capacities. You're a wretched beast. Yet, presently it's my chance to make you endure." It shouted at him. Its back mouth went after him. He hurled himself far removed. Becoming stained with the blood of the room.

It stepped its hands and feet. Making the ground shake. He staggered back. Getting his foot. He terminated at its appearances. It raised its appendages. Shouting at the aggravation. A portion of its appendages isolates from itself. Running or jumping towards him. He kicked some while stepping others. It raised one of its feet. Focusing on him. He lost his grasp on the weapon. Hurling himself to the side.

The firearm disintegrated into pieces at its solidarity. He took out his shotgun. Terminating beneath it. Tearing through its tissue. It shouted out. Imploding on the ground. He pulled the trigger however the firearm was unfilled. He tossed it to the side. Advancing toward the animal. He kicked it. "Simply pass on as of now! Nobody needs you! I don't require you!" The back mouth's arm got him. He hammered his clench hands against it. "No! Let me go! God damn it!"

Despite the fact that he felt alone, he swore there was more than one presence. As though his new companions were here. Something in his mind advised him to utilize the container.

He hauled it out. Tossing the container of pills in there once he was sufficiently close. The hand dropped him. He hit the ground. Jumping. Cleaned Crawler thrashed around. Experiencing in extraordinary torment as it shouted. He slithered away from it. Watching its tissue move in such weird bearings. Unfit to keep a steady structure. Its body became increasingly large until it detonated.

He covered his face with his arm. Protecting himself from the many body parts that had landed. He jumped at an unexpected aggravation. He saw his arm. Seeing a cut on his sleeve which some blood. It was a little cut yet it actually confused him that the animal had the option to get him all things considered.

His eyes squinted.

Kevin sat before the town's sign. He wound up holding the keys to a bike that sat close by. He sat on it. Firing it up prior to heading out. He grinned at the dawn. Realizing that it actually hurt however that he may as yet grin. That he could improve things.

That he could be his own legend.

The End...